Gala Dominic is the pseudonym of a young writer from the Dominican Republic, who was born and raised in a small provincial town in Central Asia, but for the sake of fulfilling her dream, she was not afraid to go alone to the other end of the world and live on a tropical island in the Caribbean.

The writer has always been surrounded by people of different nationalities and cultures, which greatly influenced the formation of her personality, her life values, and a special understanding of the world.

The adventures of Gala herself formed the basis of many plots of this fantasy book, where the author shares her experiences with the readers through the characters of the story.

Gala Dominic

TIME TO SPREAD WINGS

AUSTIN MACAULEY PUBLISHERS™

LONDON • CAMBRIDGE • NEW YORK • SHARJAH

Ordering Information
Quantity sales: Special discounts are available on quantity purchases by corporations, associations, and others. For details, contact the publisher at the address below.

Publisher's Cataloging-in-Publication data
Dominic, Gala
Time to Spread Wings

ISBN 9798889107620 (Paperback)
ISBN 9798889107637 (ePub e-book)

Library of Congress Control Number: 2023920554

www.austinmacauley.com/us

First Published 2024
Austin Macauley Publishers LLC
40 Wall Street, 33rd Floor, Suite 3302
New York, NY 10005
USA

mail-usa@austinmacauley.com
+1 (646) 5125767

Table of Contents

The heroes of this magic book were born special: fate gave them wings. And, like any gift from above, these wings determined the destiny of the four friends forever – to be the first to help people in trouble. The heroes act as a team of desperate rescuers, ready for anything and risking their lives for others.

Time to Spread Wings is the first book in a trilogy. A stormy whirl of events brings the main character Gela either to the high-mountainous Pamir or to the tropical Dominican Republic. She will have to believe in herself, find true friends, and go through the difficult path to fight evil.

The fabulous trilogy of adventures of Gela and her friends is an attempt by the young author Gala Dominic to remind the world of the most important things for every person: courage and bravery, friendship and mutualism, kindness and bright goals. Each of the three books written in the fantasy genre reflects the true values of real people, as it to a great extent resonates with events from the writer's life.

Prologue

The variety of colors and fragrances of Moscow Airport reminded me of a spring meadow. As bluets carelessly neighbored with widow grass so the smell of stuffed potatoes mingled with fragrances of fancy make-up store.

I had to stay a little longer than usual at the arrival and departure board to locate the check-in desk for Punta Cana – after all, this was the first flight I had to take. Being in the departure hall, when I had a couple of free minutes left, I decided to drop into the WC – no, not to touch up my makeup (I didn't use it) – I just wanted to make sure that nothing could be viewed under my blouse. I cautiously examined myself from behind in a large mirror. The blouse sat perfectly on a straight back. "OK," I reassured myself. And took a deep breath as I heard the passengers being announced to board the Moscow-Punta Cana flight. Going up the stairs, in my mind I said goodbye to everything that I was leaving behind. I had a 12-hour transatlantic flight waiting for me. I'd never been in the air for so long, but the iron wings seemed quite reliable to take me to a new life.

I made myself comfortable in the seat of the place, fastened my seat belt and grabbed a book. But under the soothing rumble of turbines, my eyes closed, and my memory took me back to the summer of 2000.

Chapter 1
My 11 'A'

GELA

It was the middle of June, and the Asian summer heat had not yet burnt out the bright crown of the trees that covered the school grounds like gracious paws. All 11 'A' guys were in, discussing the upcoming graduation ball. See that tall slim girl with a book in her hands? That's me – Gela Agapi. Reading is my passion. It doesn't matter what the book is about, whether it's a thrilling detective story or a painting works manual. As soon as I learned to read, no one could ever imagine me without a book, I swallowed them right on the go.

Having my eyes glued on the book, I came up to a group of my classmates. Hearing their loud voices and seeing their desperate gestures, it is not difficult to guess that again they were proving to each other the rightness of their choice. For some time now, this issue has been noticeably on the agenda.

"What is it all about?" I asked just for the sake of courtesy.

"I say that artificial intelligence can't replace painting, music and, generally, high art in the modern world. People will always need artists, just like they need economists and lawyers," Anna was trying to convince her opponents. She had remarkable painting abilities, one of her paintings was even hung on the wall in the principal's office, and she had a future plan to win a scholarship for studying at the famous art college in New York.

"Oh, come on! Nowadays, you don't need to move across the canvas with a brush to capture a wonderful moment, it's just enough to use a special app that will create any picture just as good as Van Gogh. Literally, it is just a matter of technology because mankind has already come up with so many gadgets to assist itself and will come up with more," our computer genius and future IT specialist Valeria was trying to convince us.

This discussion could become a never-ending story. Right from the first grade, they found a lot of reasons for arguing, each standing on her own opinion. And it seemed like the dispute about eternal beauty and rational reality did not have a simple answer by any stretch. Everyone has long been making boasts about where everyone was planning to get admitted. But not me. I wasn't in a rush to tell everyone about my choice, something was like holding me back. Since my childhood, I had my own secret that nobody was supposed to know about. My secret made me a clam. Many have given me up not trying to draw out.

"And what do you think, eternal dumb dog?" Anna asked me cockily.

"Oh hell no. Don't get me into this. And besides, it's time to go now, the rehearsal has already begun, and we will be left with the clumsiest boys in the class."

We rushed to the school, leaving all disputes behind. 11-'A' grade was rehearsing a waltz; it was the very dance that was supposed to solemnly open our graduation ball.

I came back home in the evening. We lived in a tiny apartment in the suburbs, just 15 minutes away from the capital. I loved this place with its twisting, like grandma's lace, backstreets, and alleys. The family was stuffed into two small rooms, one bedroom was shared by me and my brother, and my mom was occupying the other. Therefore, the kitchen was our special place at home. It always smelled of different goodies; it was the place where we were coming together every day for dinner to share the events of the past day.

"How are the rehearsals going?" mom shouted from the kitchen, not interrupting her cooking. "Didn't your boys trample your feet?"

"Hey! Mmm, what smells so yummy!?" I asked her, instead of replying trying to see what was in the pan over my mother's shoulder. "Our boys began to fall into step more often, but it is still yet impossible to call it a dance. We are more like tumbler dolls," I said without much enthusiasm, wondering to myself how this wild idea to dance the waltz came to us who were brought up on completely different rhythms.

"Wash your hands, your hungry brother is tired of waiting for you. By the way, I stepped into the post office today, you have mail. Look at your desk with the books," scattered my mother.

I went into the room and took the envelope. The letter was from the Academy of Tourism.

"Tourism…it's definitely not for me," flashed through my mind. All our life, we have never gone further than to the capital's market for shopping. Well, we were also mobilized as a class to harvest tomatoes last year. But this is also not tourism. When I opened the letter, I read:

"Dear applicant Gela Agapi, we are pleased to announce that you have been admitted to the 1st year program of the Academy of Tourism. Please visit the academy to obtain the learning materials on June 28, room 300."

I looked at the sheet of paper in bewilderment from all sides: the date, the seal, and even someone's illegible signature – everything was just as it should be in an official letter.

I went back to the kitchen in complete confusion.

"Mom, there must be a mistake. They messed something up. The letter is not intended for me. I did not apply to the Academy of Tourism. Probably someone is waiting for this letter instead of me. What do I do now?" I was completely confused.

Mom ran her hand along my back, either stroking or straightening it. She did this when I was very young. Mom already knew then that in moments of emotional excitement, there, in the shoulder blades, a kind of special stirring begins inside of me. She revealed that secret from the very beginning. But she's never discussed it with anyone.

Even with me.

After making sure that everything was in order, my mother took the envelope from my hands and calmly said, pointing to the address:

"My dear, I think you need to go there and find it out."

"Yes, I will do that tomorrow, without waiting for the 28th."

"Now let's get to dinner at last!"

Chapter 2
Unexpected Invitation

I've been looking for the Tourism Academy building for quite a while: I've never been to this part of the city before. And even when I found the mentioned address, I still did not believe that I got to the right place: with its mirrored façade, this skyscraper looked more like a modern office than an education place. Only after reading the sign at the entrance, I stumblingly half-opened the massive door. The spacious lobby was deserted, my steps were muffled only by the AC noise. It felt like there was not a single soul in the building. Suddenly, from somewhere out of the depth of the cloakroom, a nimble old woman appeared and strictly asked:

"What are you doing here? What is your issue?"

I mumbled something about a mistake with the addressee, pointing at the letter. The concierge was clearly not in a mood for long talk: kindly, but at the same time quite insistently, she took me out of the door, adding:

"Come at the appointed time, my dear. Come on the 28th and sort it all out."

Afterdays passed in the fuss of exams and preparation for the graduation ball. June 28th showed up unexpectedly fast. The familiar building externally still looked like an office, but inside it was by no means a quiet piece of glass. Concerned young people scurried up and down the stairs, the elevator cabins were constantly moving up and down. Now the building looked like a smashed beehive – Tourism Academy was full of such a diverse public. In contrast to the general fuss, a group of girls stood out just as if they had just stepped off the cover of a fashion magazine. It seemed like they were the only ones not disturbed by this turmoil, they were clearly fascinated by the discussion of outfits. Not so far from them, like a nonintersecting planet, a group of students bustled about, sorting out camping equipment. Suddenly, the tent went out of control and began to unfold right in the lobby. To my great surprise, fashion girls rushed to help the guys. They acted very confidently and, with the agility of tiger tamers, coped with the monster tent joking with their unlucky classmates without malice. Meanwhile, I kept on moving to my goal trying not to stare around. I had to find classroom 300.

It wasn't difficult. Going up above the lobby, I easily climbed several stairways, circled under the ceiling on several floors, and finally found the door I needed. I quietly sat in a chair near the office – so that the group of guys sitting next to it did not notice how I ended up next to them.

"Who is for No. 300?" I asked uncertainly.

The first to answer, recovering from my sudden appearance, was a sonorous girl, looking more like an elf with pointy ears, tousled curls and acid-purple lipstick on her lips. The elf look was completed with a colorfully printed denim jacket and shorts with skinny knees sticking out from under them.

"I'm Yuka. Now they will start calling up," she said confidently.

"Gela," I introduced myself to either the elf girl or the whole group. There was no reaction from the guys, and I began to look at them curiously.

But I couldn't keep my eyes on the other girl. She was constantly moving from one place to another, putting her ear to the door – and immediately bouncing off it like a scalded one. At the same time, she constantly muttered something. I listened and caught that she was naming the highest peaks in the world. I was getting convinced more and more that the letter wrongly appeared at my address.

"And I was going to become a pilot. They didn't admit me because of my ears: weak ears can't bear the pressure drops at altitude," said the elf girl with the potato's name.

"Who would have thought that it was your ears that would let you down?" the guy remarked with undisguised irony, not showing up any excitement. He was a bit arrogant. Looking at everyone, like a bird from the height of his flight, he demonstrated with all his appearance that he knew what he was worthy of. He was handsome with the standard beauty that blows the mind of any girl: tall, athletic, with pumped-up muscles looking out through a thin shirt. And a look that was hypnotizing and frightening at the same time. There was something predatory in him. I preferred to stay away from such guys.

The waiting time was incredibly long. They called up to the room one by one. Finally, my turn come. I found myself in a spacious bright room – as if I had flown into it. Nothing superfluous, only a desk with a PC and an armchair on the opposite side – apparently for the visitors. A woman whose age was difficult to determine at first glance was sitting at the desk.

"Gela, sit down," she said friendly, nodding at the chair. Her voice was soothing, like a mountain spring. But the age was not determined even at a second glance. "My name is Marina Alekseyevna, you can call me simply Marina. You are probably confused because of the letter you've received, are you?"

I didn't even have time to say hello. That woman filled all the free space with herself, forcing me to focus only on herself.

"I know you didn't apply. We ourselves decided to invite you to study. I must confess we rarely come across people like you, with an unusual hunger for knowledge and knowledge in all fields. I spotted you two years ago at the Literature Olympiad. Your work impressed me with the originality and non-standard solutions," continued Marina. "I ask you not to refuse to study at the Academy. I'm sure you won't regret it. Along with the standard program in the specialty, you will have the opportunity to study philosophy and etiquette, not to mention foreign languages. And everything is free. You don't have to pass any exams, I saw your high school diploma. Don't miss your chance! Well, for what it's worth, you can always transfer to another university to become a librarian in the end. Do you really dream of it? I offer to make another choice. It's time to spread your wings," she finished.

I was shocked by her knowledge of my school grades and plans for admission: it looked like she was watching me and knew about my secret. At the same time, I really wanted to sit in the classrooms where they teach philosophy and etiquette.

I left the office in thoughts and reached home automatically. The phrase, "It's time to spread your wings," which Marina conspiratorially uttered at the end, settled in my head.

I told my mother about the results of my visit to the Academy and about my confusion. Surprisingly, my mother also supported the idea of studying there. A prestigious university, not everyone manages to get there – it was my mother who did her 'homework' and found out everything about the Academy. She did not like long instructions, considering me already an adult girl. She just wisely remarked, "Do not be afraid to use the chance that the Universe gives you. Your home is just a starting point where you can always return. Never give up on changes in your life."

I went to bed after midnight; my brother snored for a long time, turning to the wall. Before putting on my pajamas and getting into bed, I went to the mirror, trying to see the wings on my back. But apart from youth acne, with which it was densely strewn, I saw nothing.

Chapter 3
Graduation Ball

Despite the fact that everyone was getting prepared for the long-awaited graduation ball, it still came up all of a sudden. I still do remember the reaction my outfit caused. I was wearing a slinky claret-color dress. It covered the body from neck to toe and at first glance, seemed very modest. But with every step, my long leg was coquettishly opened by a high slit, framed by a fringe. The entire dress was embroidered with pearls. Nobody would ever guess that my mother and I sewed this dress by a pattern taken from an old fashion magazine. I had to sacrifice our ancestral tablecloth and my mother's only pearl necklace. My hair was parted in the middle and pinned up at the top, and my eyes were lined with thin arrows a-la Audrey Hepburn. Even the best friends stood speechless.

Anna woke up first, confessing that she barely recognized me:

"Is it really you, sister?! We thought you wouldn't trade your 'blue stocking' style for anything. You look gorgeous!"

The solemn speech of the director and his baccalaureate sermon made the girls distract from my new image. The teachers wished us great achievements, the parents brushed away their tears, and the newly made graduates were overwhelmed with emotions. Even the waltz was a success: it was worth torturing our boys for so long. The adults clapped their hands in emotion, and the performers looked around in the hope that the older generation would finally disappear, leaving them on their own.

The night went through in such a frenzied fun as if we were leaving forever our bunch of bumps and mistakes made before. At dawn, we snapped back to reality. Everyone froze, staring at the melting stars in the sky. Apparently, this is how childhood goes. Almost simultaneously, everyone started talking about the future – who plans to go where. I remember my classmates' rounded eyes when I said that I was admitted to the Tourism Academy.

Only Valeria squeezed out of herself, "You know, I thought your prom dress would be on the top of conversation for the next five years, and now you're giving out another shocking news! So, it turns out that you betrayed your dream?"

"No, I've simply changed my dream!" I replied with confidence.

Chapter 4
Fantastic Four

And so, the day X came – the first day at the Academy. For the uninitiated, the fuss of the noisy mass of students reminded me of the great chaos. In fact, it all made perfect sense. By their overgrown beards, heavy backpacks, and scraps of phrases about long trips, one could easily guess seniors. They spoke a little louder than necessary about their summer travel experiences, trying to impress not only their girlfriends but everyone around them. In contrast to the confident-looking school old-timers, it was easy to guess the newcomers, who had yet to live their travel adventures. The freshmen hugged the walls, and each of them felt alone in the seething crowd: no acquaintances, no common topics to chat on. Finally, we were all invited into a great hall.

I appeared to sit next to Yuka. Probably, I intuitively went to the 'beacon' in a floral denim jacket. Another girl sat down with us, whom I met when I first visited the Academy. The handsome sat in front. He looked back and winked – it seemed to everyone at once, but it seemed to every girl that this secret sign was addressed exclusively to her alone. My neighbors were delighted with such personal attention, and both simultaneously blushed either from embarrassment or from pleasure. For me, this wink of this over self-confident guy caused nothing but irritation.

After a general information briefing, Marina approached and invited us into her office. It was already familiar to us, but a sofa was new in the interior. The girls and I sat down on it, closely clinging to each other so that there was enough seat for Alex as well. Looking ahead, I will note that both this office and the sofa will become dear to us during our studies at the Academy. We will spend a lot of time here, even when Marina herself is not with us.

"Glad to see you again," Marina said. "You might have already known each other. What do you mean 'No'?" she wondered, noticing our confusion. "Well then, let's fix this. Gela, Yuka, Ninel, and Alex," Marina said encouragingly, looking into everyone's eyes. "And I will be your mentor while you study at the Academy. Part of the time, you will study according to the general time-schedule, but you will also have special disciplines that are not available to everyone. These are a variety of subjects – they should come in handy for you to cope with unusual situations. And believe me, there will be many of such in your life."

And she handed us a sheet with a list of disciplines, which we began to look at with curiosity in order to digest the cherished list.

"You already possess some skills that distinguish you from the rest of your peers. My task is to teach you how to apply these skills of yours in practice."

How strange, I thought. Frankly, I have always considered myself the most ordinary girl, an ordinary person. What is it about me that differs me from others?

And what are these superpowers of which I am unaware? There were only questions in my head and no answers.

Probably, needless to say that our four aroused bewilderment not only among our classmates. Well, what could a nerd, an elf girl, a goth, and the 'Brad Pitt' of the whole class have in common? It was a usual thing for the place we appeared at to label people, and so, the nickname 'Fantastic Four' quickly stuck with us. But we didn't really mind. We really stood out from the general class of students. The elf girl, or, as Yuka was called for her ears and love of lilac lipstick, 'a stranger from space,' was kind and sympathetic. She had an amazing ability to be where she was most needed, and a rare ability to organize and involve everyone in any activity. Anyone could go with her without any fear both to a disco party and to the military reconnaissance task.

The goth girl, i.e. Ninel, really always dressed in all black. But her smile and eternal positive gave others so much light and energy that when she entered (or rather burst into) the audience, no one noticed the mournful shade of her outfit. Moreover, clothes of this color perfectly emphasized her jet-black hair.

Well, Brad Pitt, who at first annoyed me so much, turned out to be a nice guy. I got warm relations with him, we were more like a brother and sister. I had a younger brother, and Alex became my older brother – you could always trust him with the most important things and, if necessary, cry on his strong shoulder. Despite the fact that we were very young, Alex had the wisdom of an old man.

I did not skip a single class and absorbed knowledge with such a thirst the African savannah absorbs rainwater with after a drought. I dressed, to tell the truth, so-so – after all, I'm a crammer, which means a blue stocking.

I preferred bulky sweaters, a couple of sizes larger than my own. It seemed to me that appearance did not matter at all: everyone should see who I am and what I represent, no matter what I wear.

I devoured every genetics book I could find. But I could not find an explanation for why my teenage acne on my back began to turn into faded chicken feathers.

Chapter 5
Moment of Truth

I still remember our moment of recognition. We were getting ready for the first exam session, and, like all other students, we were terrified of exams. Along with the main disciplines, we had to take one more of the subjects that we studied additionally. What kind of subject it would be, no one really knew. Each of us was supposed to find it out right at the exam itself. But I didn't worry about additional disciplines. I learned and read everything that was required (and even more than that), with the same enthusiasm. My pain was only a foreign language. It seemed to me that my English professor didn't like me from the very beginning. I didn't understand anything he was trying to convey to us.

My brain refused to perceive the material in his lectures. And after classes, Yuka explained everything to me in a simple, accessible language, so that the lessons themselves fit into my head in the right order. This is how I imagined the structure of my brain: like in a library, all the information is sorted into shelves and into the necessary sections. The guys constantly made fun of me – they say, get the book from the right shelf.

Ninel often asked how I managed to keep order in my head. There is no less information in her chambers of the mind, but she could not get the right one at the right time. I promised to teach her.

As usual, we gathered at Yuk's house: she lived closest to the Academy, and her dad got used to our hanging out at their place. Yuki's home was as eclectic as herself. The walls of the room were covered with photo wallpapers of pastoral landscapes, and the wallpapers featured huge posters of her favorite rock stars. There was a lamp in the shape of a skull on the desktop near the computer. At the same time, there was a flowered children's carpet on the floor – on it, we settled down with our textbooks. And sequins, sequins everywhere. The sequins were scattered all over the apartment. Yuka's dad deserves a separate story: he is an amazing person and looks very much like Yuka – or rather, Yuka looks like him.

But, unlike his daughter, he only had a pointed left ear. He raised her alone. We never asked a friend what happened to her mother, and she preferred to remain silent.

Dad was a jack of all trades. He helped us understand some of the home tasks and periodically treated us to pastries that he made himself. This time, he knocked on the door right in time, apparently, feeling that we needed to have a break.

"Children, I baked buns for you. Come on, grab them!"

We didn't have to be persuaded. Quickly jumping up from the carpet, we took a tray with tea and fresh buns – a real salvation for the brain boiling from learning.

"Thanks! This is what we need."

He delicately closed the door behind him.

"Gela, don't you think it's time to stop sleeping on other people's pillows?" Yuka asked, narrowing her eyes to slits so that it was impossible to tell if she was joking or serious.

"What do you mean? What pillows?" I wondered.

"Well, that's what they say when they find feathers on a person's clothes. Look." She pointed to the seat where I had just been sitting.

There were not only feathers but also fluff. The view was as if a goose was butchered in this place. I tried to turn the conversation into a joke:

"I think it will be useful for the Christmas toys that you make in your free time."

It was Yuki's turn to be surprised now.

"What toys?"

"Well, aren't all these sequins in your apartment for Christmas tree decoration?"

And while Yuka thought about what to say in response, and the others waited, as if pressing the pause, I felt that there would be no better opportunity.

"Guys, I have to tell you something. Or rather, show."

I took off my huge sweater and turned my back to them. Between the shoulder blades, small wings protruded, like those of a barely fledged chicken.

"Well, something like this... I carry my 'pillows' with me."

Yuka was the first to break the silence.

"So, you've got angel wings, haven't you? Oh wow!"

"Well, I would not call it so loudly 'angel wings.' Do you see them at all?" I objected.

"So why the hell do I have this?" Yuka jumped up abruptly, took off her jacket with a jerk, turned around – and I saw the wings of a dragonfly. They were folded along her back – insanely beautiful, transparent, shimmering with all the colors of the rainbow.

"Oh, so, it's not the very fact of having wings that confuse you but only how they look?" I was surprised.

Alex couldn't take it anymore. He stood between us with the phrase 'Girls, don't fight' and strangely shrugged his shoulders. At the same moment, huge grey wings opened up to our gaze, unfolding behind him.

Ninel, looking at all this madness with goggle eyes, quietly said, "It seems to me that Yuki's dad overplayed with the recipe of buns."

Now everyone was looking at her, expecting her to show us something. Alex even encouraged, "Come on, Ninel, surprise us. What do you have behind your back?"

"Nothing. Absolutely nothing."

We did not believe it, pulled off her sweater, began to twist in all directions, but really found nothing. No hint of wings.

Then Yuka and I attacked Alex with questions. Finally, there was someone who was able to explain at least something.

Chapter 6
From Rescuers' Caste

"How?! Where?! Why?!" interrupting each other, we hurried to get answers from Alex. "Where did he get such gorgeous wings? How to manage them? Why are our wings so different?"

"Well, ladies, you want too much from me," Alex said it so calmly as if it was about the most ordinary things. Taking each of us by the shoulders and seating us one by one, he calmly remarked, "You have to figure out yourself where your 'wingedness' comes from. But I am ready to tell you my story – perhaps you will find the tips you need in it."

ALEX

I, like all my ancestors, was born and raised in a remote mountain village. The elders claimed that the great Genghis Khan stopped in this area on his way to conquer the world. Our people are hunters-rescuers, and luck in this business has always been and remains on our side. It is clear that now there is no urgent need to hunt for food, but we have not forgotten all the steep paths, and we are well aware of the habits of wild animals that live on the edge of our mountains and forests. Many of my fellow tribesmen received special education in the cities – they returned to their native places and conducted tours for lovers of extreme tourism, for those who want to see the rare world of wildlife and exotic animals, mostly listed in the Red Book, with their own eyes. At the same time, they do not forget about another age-old duty – to protect travelers. Ordinary hunting with rifles and firing at live targets stays in the past, now it has been replaced by photo hunting. But it also requires special training.

From an early age, we, the children of hereditary hunters, help adults. In winter, the boys repair equipment, and from the age of 14, fathers begin to take them along to accompany groups of travelers. My life little differed from the life of my peers. But not everyone in our village has wings. Such children are born once every fifty years, and no one knows when and with whom the winged heir will be born. And so it happened that such an heir appeared in my family. I am the only child of my parents, and from an early age, I had a great responsibility – in due time I should become a conductor of the skills accumulated by generations and a teacher to the young guys following me.

Apart from special skills, such a legend has been passed from mouth to mouth for many centuries. Our clan of nomads has lived in the Tien Shan since the beginning of time. And then one day, having fallen into a terrible hurricane, they got lost and for a long time could not find their way among the avalanches that came down from the mountains. They walked in circles: it seemed as if the evil spirits were deliberately confusing the way out for them. There was no food, the cold fettered the body. Being on the verge of death, people turned to the prophet with a plea for help. And he showed his grace and sent a falcon to help them. The falcon taught the nomads how to hunt and find the right paths but took a promise from them that they would always save all those who got lost in those mighty mountains and open the beauty of the Tien Shan to those who wanted to touch it.

"But how, Lord, will we find these paths without your messenger?" the nomads asked.

"I am granting you a guide who will be born once every fifty years. He will be rewarded with wings and endowed with the bravery, courage, and vigilance of a falcon."

And so it happened that once every fifty years, a man with wings was born and was trained by the previous guide.

And from my very birth, in addition to ordinary knowledge, I received additional ones – the precepts of my ancestors, if I may say. Of course, one of my first questions was, "What if strangers see me? After all, many tourists flock to us in the summer season, especially recently. The now fashionable wave of ecotourism brings here different people who are able to shell out big money to see the snow leopard Irbis or the Marco Polo Mountain sheep."

The elder narrowed his eyes slyly and replied, "Young man, most people do not see the obvious things that are happening right under their noses. Even if you open your wings during rush hour on the subway, the most they will feel is that they have become cramped. Don't worry. They will open only when you need them. To find a path, take a trail, save a man…"

I didn't know then what a 'subway' or 'rush hour' meant, but I could not doubt the words of the elder.

Shaken by Alex's story, we sat in silence. But not for long: soon questions again rained down:

"It is not clear how you got into the Academy. And why do you need it, if your fate as a rescue guide has already been decided?"

"It all started with Marina. Last year, she ended up in our mountains. A group of tourists, including Marina, wanted to see a live snow leopard at all costs. I had to be their guide. As soon as I took the leopard trail in the mountains, my wings spread. But I didn't worry that someone might see them. This happened to me not for the first time, and those around me always behaved completely calmly, not suspecting me of something unusual. But there was something in Marina's eyes from which I understood:

she sees them. She did not give herself away, but when we returned to the village, she immediately asked to be taken to the yurt of the elders. I complied with the request, although I was sure that they would not talk to her. However, I was wrong. Entering the yurt, Marina made a greeting gesture with her hands, and the elders answered her in the same way. I note that I have never seen them greet any of the strangers with such a gesture before. It was a sign of crossed hands, clasped thumbs."

Alex showed us this sign.

"It looks like how my mother folded her hands when we played shadow theatre with her as a child," flashed through my head.

"Go on," I implored Alex impatiently.

"It was at that moment that I was kicked out of the yurt. I had to obey." Alex sighed.

"It's hard to believe that you were a very obedient boy!" Yuka noticed.

"And you are absolutely right! But, you know, it's hard to eavesdrop at a yurt where there are no corners and still be unnoticed." I could only hear parts of phrases, but it was impossible to make out what exactly they were talking about. Then my father called me, and I was forced to leave this place. But my curiosity was satisfied that evening. My parents and I were invited to the elders, and the verdict was passed. The elders announced that as soon as I graduated from school, I would immediately go to study in the city. Marina-ezhe (which was the proper way to address an honorable guest) convinced them that a special boy like me should get an education that was in line with modern trends. At the same time, it was wisely noted that the school in our village had not been updated for decades. Its graduates, of course, can read and write, and have the skills necessary for life in our region, but many have never left beyond it throughout their lives, while the big world around us has noticeably changed. And since, upon reaching the age of 21, I was to take a place in the yurt of elders, they considered it foolish to deny the future leader the opportunity to receive an education. Moreover, Marina-ezhe assured that they would not have to bear any expenses. This became the final argument.

My parents did not dare to object to the authoritative elders, so my future was determined in just five minutes. After school, I was equipped to study at the Tourism Academy, and after graduation, I must return to my native village.

Leaving the yurt, I nevertheless asked the elders, "Does she know? Did she see them?"

The short answer was yes, but don't worry about it. My task is not to disgrace our family and to accept all the knowledge that will be given.

"Here is a short story about how I got into the Academy. Here I immediately realized that you are not simple vixens. And I even asked Marina if she knows what you are. To which I was told that there is a time for everything. And she will answer all questions when you are ready to ask them," Alex concluded.

"Well, I don't see any reason to put this conversation off," Yuka blurted out, jumping up from the floor. "Let's go to Marina for answers!"

We immediately moved to the Academy.

Chapter 7
Hard to Believe in a Fairy Tale

Extremely excited, we flew into Marina's office. We were deeply impatient to get answers to the questions that have been tormenting each of us for so long. She left her desk, greeting us with the gesture that Alex mentioned. That puzzled us so much that we stopped dead, looking at each other.

Unlocking her hands, Marina pointed to the sofa. We dutifully sat down in our usual places.

"I see you want to ask me something. Apparently, it's time to tell who you are and why you are so special," said Marina.

Her voice had a calming effect on us, as it always did. But there was nothing more important than to know the whole truth about yourself. We started bombarding her with questions. In this hubbub, which looked more like the cries of chicks, it was difficult to make out anything intelligible.

"So, let's go one by one and start with a greeting." By joining my hands with a sign symbolizing the wingspan, I seem to say, "I know. I see. I accept." And then the owner of the wings will no longer be afraid that I will betray their secret and can always count on help. In my life, I have seen a lot of winged people, there are many more of them than you think.

"By accepting yourself as you are, you will learn to see the wings of others. Some have them quite prominent," said Marina and looked at Yuka. "And others still have to believe in themselves to feel them behind their backs," she added, looking at Ninel.

"As you have already noticed, everyone's wings are different. Of course, you are interested in what it depends on. And it depends on your destiny, on the karmic debt to the family," Marina explained. "After all, we are all born for a reason and come to this world for different purposes. I confess I've never had wings. I am of the caste of guides," she continued. "We see people like you and help them find their way. We help to open up, to spread the wings for a high flight. For instance, Yuki's father, whom I have known since childhood. Don't be surprised," she looked at Yuka,

"I knew your mother too. Their relationship developed right in front of me. It seemed that those people would be infinitely happy. But a tragedy struck: Yuki's mother passed away at her birth. I'm sorry, girl, I don't want to hurt you, but you know how hard your father suffered this tragedy. It was a strong blow for your dad: not only did he lose his love – he lost himself. And his wings. All he was left with was a helpless little baby. He put all his love and care into his daughter, into you, Yuka. When your wings began to appear – and this happened a couple of years ago – you firmly decided that travel would become the meaning of your life. More than anything, you wanted to discover new countries and unknown worlds. You vaguely understood that this desire had something to do with the wings growing behind your shoulders, didn't you?"

"Indeed," Yuka stunned and whispered. "Dad said that one day I'll find out everything, but for now, we must keep my unusualness a secret."

"Right. Then your dad came to me. He was at a loss and did not know how to explain to you why you feel in yourself something that is not in others. After all, many years ago, I helped him to accept his wings. Your father asked me to help you too. I promised that I would do it when the time comes."

"But why does Alex have such gorgeous bird wings, and I have some dragonfly-like?!" Yuka flared again.

"Because you are descendants of different families. Do you have any idea of who your ancestor was?" asked Marina slyly narrowing her eyes.

"Umm… A dragonfly?" Yuka said. "I really hope that at least not the one from the fairy tale who 'slept lazily all summer…'"

"Ha, close, but not quite. Elves. Your ancestors were elves," Marina replied.

"Are you trying to say that I am related to the elves from the fairy tales?" Yuka asked incredulously.

We sat on the couch, huddled close to each other and not daring to interfere in their dialogue. It's time for Yuki, the girl from the land of the elves.

"I must say that sometimes, life is full of things that you wouldn't find in any fairy tale," Marina emphasized, referring mainly to Yuka. "And fairy tales are not always just idle fantasies. Often, they are based on legends. And legends, as you know, are made up of life realities. They are passed from mouth to mouth, from generation to generation. So, if you're ready, I'll tell you your legend."

YUKA

"The roots of your family, Yuka, go back to those ancient times when forests covered most of our planet." Elves and druids lived in those forests, guarded them, took care of them – and received generous gifts from them, allowing local inhabitants to use some part of them as well. Gloomy, grumpy druids lived in the very depth of those forests. Elves, on the other hand, bright winged creatures, real spirits of the forest, occupied the flower meadows. They tirelessly gathered berries, mushrooms, and herbs, made various medicinal infusions from them and much more, devoting their lives to what later became known as folk medicine. It is no coincidence that the inhabitants of nearby villages applied to the healers with fantastic knowledge. Some needed an ointment to heal a wound, and some needed a magical spell for a loved one.

But time passed through, centuries passed, and eras changed. People mercilessly cut down trees and destroyed forests, reducing the green divine gift. At first, elves, under the guise of healers, lived among people, but as civilization conquered the world more and more, the need for them vanished. And only in the last few decades, humanity has acutely felt the lack of fresh breath, and simple life on earth

– and decided to return to the origins, to mother nature, or, as they say now, to an ecological lifestyle. In addition, people are increasingly paying attention to the composition of a particular medical product, whether it be pain pills or a beauty product. Everyone wants them to be based on herbs, essential, natural elements. Those who knew many secrets of the earth have become urgently needed. And so, the elves began to revive. This also happened in Yuki's father's family. His parents, that is, your grandfather and grandmother, long before the birth of their winged boy, mastered, like everyone in their family, the profession of a biologist. From generation to generation, the family passed on not only knowledge about nature and its possibilities but also a particularly sensitive, caring attitude towards people. This quality is also almost lost in the modern world, which is why the legendary elves have become so popular."

"So you want to say that I come from those very ones?" Yuka asked in bewilderment.

"At least that explains your love for floral print," I remarked trying to defuse the tension and find some reasonable explanation for Yuki's behavior.

"Now it's clear why you make us watch the bud for hours, as if it's not a flower that is blooming but a new life, and everyone is obliged to see it," Ninel supported my ironic tone.

"We thought you were just crazy, but it turns out that these are the genes of your ancestors," Alex did not miss the opportunity to tease Yuka also.

"Although…my father treats everything with herbs – and he taught me also. It seemed to me that he, as a biologist, is so passionate about his work, but here such a turn!" Yuka said puzzled, ignoring our barbs, and immediately turned to Marina again.

"Then why didn't I get drawn into biology, since the call of the ancestors is so strong?"

"What motivated you and what filled your heart? You know this better than anyone else," Marina snapped categorically.

Yuki's pointy ears twitched slightly, as they always did when she got excited.

"You know that our country is rich in rare alpine species of flowers. For example, the Aigul flower: it sprouts for seven whole years and adds a flower to its stem every seven years. There is also Edelweiss – it is called the flower of winners. Only those who have reached the top of the mountain will be able to see it."

Oh, this is going to take a lot of time, I thought instinctively. When Yuka started talking about plants so enthusiastically, it was impossible to stop her. Suddenly, I noticed her wings began to shimmer with all the colors of the rainbow. I have never seen anything like that before. And then I realized that this was happening not only because she was hiding them but also because our friend's wings were only now beginning to open for real.

We exchanged glances with Alex and Ninel, not daring to interrupt Yuka.

"Dad told me a story once," she continued. "If you collect flowers from the seven peaks of seven-thousand-meter peaks, then you can make an elixir – not eternal youth but one that will help to cope with any ailment. I guess it sounds fantastic so far. But I believe it is possible. I want to find as many components as possible to create it. Even if my elixir can only cure half of the diseases in the world, I will not give up on this venture.”

Yuki’s eyes burned with excitement, and we realized that it wouldn’t be the right moment for jokes and digs.

“So you answered your own question, why you were drawn to travel, why you decided to go in for tourism. After all, climbing to a height is only possible for those who are prepared,” Marina said. “This is your destiny, and the whole Universe will help you.”

“But how to operate them?” Yuka turned around, pointing at her wings.

“Believe in yourself, in your chosenness, and they will begin to open up. This is not a piece of advice, it is a guide to action,” the mentor said harshly and looked around at everyone, as if emphasizing that those words were addressed to each of us.

Chapter 8
Quiet Angel Flew In

"Yuka seems to be sorted out. And what about me? Why do I only have what looks like wings? It feels like an enchanted chicken pecked at me as a child and now these feathers are coming out of me. This is just painful to watch!" I abruptly took off my sweater and defiantly turned my back on Marina. And then I felt her close to me. She firmly grabbed my shoulders and began to straighten my stumps with her hands. At that moment, it was as if an electric charge pierced my body because no one had touched them before, even myself.

"Well, growth is going much faster than I expected," Marina said thoughtfully. "It definitely makes me happy."

From zero – and such a result in just a few months. Good girl! "Mmm, maybe you can explain to me what it is and how to get rid of it, in the end, can't you?" I twisted my head, trying to turn it 180 degrees.

"Are you sure you want to get rid of them?" Marina asked sternly, turning me to face her and looking intently into my eyes.

It was extremely embarrassing and hard to bear this look of hers: it seemed to penetrate into the most secret corners of my soul.

"Honestly, I'm not sure anymore. Alex handles his own ones easily. Yes, and Yuka, I see, has been living with them for a long time. If the guys succeed, they will teach me also."

"Bingo! Now you understand that all of you are here for a reason, don't you? Including you, Ninel – do not deny he obvious. Everyone, absolutely everyone."

"Forgive me, Marina," I interrupted the mentor with my usual perseverance and desire to get to the very essence, "but what will happen to me? Yuki and Alex have their own stories, and it's more or less clear what awaits them in the future. But will these grow?" I waved my hands behind my back.

"It doesn't look like wings yet, I agree. But can't you imagine what they might become?" Marina asked instead of answering.

"Well, since they already exist, I want big, white, and fluffy ones. Like those that angels are depicted with," I dreamed on.

"So, you said the key words!" Marina pushed me to the right thought.

"White and fluffy?" I wondered. "But that doesn't suit my character at all!"

"You said 'angels,'" the mentor clarified.

"Oh come on now!" Yuka couldn't resist. "Someone gets wings, as expected, with feathers! What about me?"

I noticed that Yuki's wings were outraged no less than herself. Either from the indignation of the hostess or from a clearly dismissive attitude towards themselves, they trembled and made a chirring sound. But, honestly, I didn't care about the worries of the dragonfly.

"Is that really true?" I asked, not believing what had happened. "Am I for angels???"

"Yes. It took me only a few minutes to understand this at our first meeting. After all, we are the Seekers. Looks like it's time for me to introduce myself. I belong to the Seeker caste. We see, recognize, and help people like you find their way. Sometimes, it takes time to determine the origin of a particular person, to find out what caste they belong to. More often, this happens with those who do not have obvious signs: at first, they seem ordinary, like everyone else. But when I saw you, Gela, there was no doubt that a descendant of angels stood in front of me. I will not hide: such people are very rare and very lucky. I was engulfed with the excitement of a hunter because I had never met any of the Angels before. The fact that I managed to persuade you to study with us is my personal small victory. I must warn you right away: your path is not easy. Serving and helping people is a heavy burden. Often, you will have to sacrifice your interests – and maybe even your life. Be sure: soon your, as you call them, 'stump' will take the desired shape. You, like others, will gain your wings. Everyone has already taken the first step, not giving up on them. You are standing at the beginning of your endlessly interesting and important way of the chosen ones."

Having said this, Marina spread her arms, inviting us to come closer, and hugged us as tightly and gently, as only the closest person can hug.

"And you, Ninel, when you are ready, you will also hear the answers to your questions. Everything has its time. Do not doubt: you are in this group for a reason," Marina encouraged our friend.

For the first time, without fear and irritation, I felt something big behind me. But we didn't have to think for a long time what kind of existence we would have with wings.

The future has come much faster than you might think.

Chapter 9
Our Hearts are in the Mountains

Meanwhile, life went on as usual. We studied a lot and spent all our free time in the mountains. This enthusiasm distinguished our four from the rest of the fellow students. Maybe because of the understanding of our destiny, or maybe the growing wings gave us more confidence – one way or another, we quickly matured, being ahead of our peers in knowledge and skills. But no matter how successful the classes in the classrooms were, our souls rushed to the mountains. There we could feel real freedom, there we became what nature created us, and we were not afraid of anything.

Usually, Ninel suggested the route, Alex was our guide, Yuka was responsible for the equipment and provisions, but I was unconditionally trusted to coordinate the actions from the first to the last step. It is no coincidence that for everyone at the Academy, we were a dream team.

We walked along the paths of the great Tien Shan, rising higher and higher and taking height after height. Clouds rolled under our feet. Somewhere at the level of four thousand meters, when the air becomes rarefied and people begin to experience a lack of oxygen, we, on the contrary, were breathing deeply, as if preparing for a flight. Alex led our procession and from time to time, shook his wings, trying to spread them to the fullest. And mine crackled under my clothes and rushed to freedom. Of course, they were still far from Alex's wings, but lately, they have become more and more beautiful and did not make me feel any discomfort. Yuka followed me. Despite the fact that this was not the first ascent, her wings clearly did not like the high altitude. They faded, and Yuki's mood visibly deteriorated. At such times, we called her Yuka-buka.

Ninel, as usual, entertained us with entertaining facts from the life of the pioneers – with an emphasis on the obstacles that they had to overcome in those distant times. However, if we got caught in rain, hail or snow, it was not much easier for us. In moments of danger, I mentally returned to my childhood and again saw myself as a home girl with a book in my hands. In extreme situations, I recalled those times with gratitude, because my knowledge, obtained from those very books, often saved our lives. So, indulging in memories, we imperceptibly approached the foot of the mountain. And then Ninel interrupted my thoughts.

"Friends, it's time to pitch the tent."

"Are you expecting bad weather?" I asked with apprehension, knowing that Ninel has the gift to accurately calculate any changes in nature – like those old women who determine bad weather by aching bones.

"No, I just got hungry," Ninel replied lightly. But something told me that this was just a red herring. Although one could also agree with the fact that only memories remained from a breakfast of quail eggs and mountain onions by the evening.

"I must admit, I was hoping to catch a hare and cook it for dinner, but only mountain goats live at such a height," Alex said regretfully.

"Well, camping time! We will get the emergency supply – macaroni – and arrange a royal dinner," Yuka said optimistically. "I'll go look for some spices around before the storm breaks," she added, glancing apprehensively at the sky.

After when I brought a poisonous root for tea, confusing it with ginger, and Ninel tried to light a kerosene stove without pouring kerosene into it, the roles in the household were assigned automatically: Alex and I were responsible for the equipment and gear, and the girls cooked the food.

In the evening, when the kilometers traveled and the hassle of our uncomplicated household was left behind, we got into the tent. Having hung a flashlight from the ceiling and each one settled in their sleeping bag, we began to play our favorite game 'Guess Ninel's wings,' for the hundredth time, with invariable pleasure, fantasizing what they could be. From the outside, our tent looked like a firefly under the dome of an endless starry sky.

In the meantime, the weather has clearly worsened. Despite our homegrown forecaster's assurances that everything would be fine, the canvas walls of our temporary shelter rattled harder and harder.

"I'll go check the fasteners," I volunteered and reluctantly got out of the heated sleeping bag.

"Wait up, I'll go with you," Ale said.

It did not escape from me that he had been acting strangely all day and seemed to be looking for an excuse to be left alone with me.

Once I got out of the tent, I immediately began to tighten the ropes. Icy gusts of wind pierced through and through, and I could not wait to finish this job. Meanwhile, the hurricane intensified, and that said, the chances that our tent would be carried away, like Ellie's house, to the fabulous Emerald City increased.

I suddenly felt a hot breath on my neck.

"Gela, we need to talk," Alex whispered in my ear.

"Can't it wait for a better moment?" I almost shouted, trying to overcome the wind.

Alex abruptly turned me to face him and spread his wings, creating a space protected from the elements. It became quiet – I could not even believe that bad weather was raging a few steps away from us. It seemed that we were alone in the universe, and this feeling involuntarily forced us to cling to each other. Alex's lips were so close that it was impossible not to touch them. I think I was the first to reach out to him. He immediately responded with a kiss. We froze, filled with new sensations.

To my surprise, the world did not shake. I just degusted this man. His lips were warm and soft. It's not that disappointing – rather, slightly surprised. Alex, who was firmly entrenched in the glory of a tough guy, was soft and helpless in the depths of his soul. It somehow immediately sobered me up, there was not a trace of excitement left. "No, it's not for me," I told myself quickly.

The moment after the kiss, when I first turned to stone and then abruptly pulled away, seemed to last forever. Alex did not let me out of his strong embrace. I put my hands on his chest, trying to build some distance between us. His heart was beating wildly under my palms. He said something about his feelings, that I suit him like no other. But my brain refused to accept these words. I was shaking my head from side to side, trying to shake off this hypnosis. Still not understanding what the person who would take my heart unconditionally would be like, I knew for sure that Alex would never become one. A reliable friend, a guy with almost no flaws. He must be lucky – with another girl. All these thoughts came to me much later, and at that moment, I abruptly pushed him away and took a step back, not caring that I would be without the protection of his wings.

I saw surprise and even admiration in Alex's eyes. He seemed to recognize me again, looking from head to toe. I followed his gaze and found that I was not left helpless: my own wings were fully extended and gave a reliable guarantee that gusts of wind would not carry me away like a light grain of sand.

I extended my hand to Alex for a friendly handshake, hoping that this awkward episode would not jeopardize our friendship. But Alex did not answer the handshake but folded his palms in a 'winged' greeting and bowed his head in acceptance of me as an equal partner.

We hid mutual awkwardness by strengthening the tent on both sides. We returned to it one after another. Alex never talked about his feelings for me again.

Chapter 10
Mission

Before we knew where we were, our last spring at the Academy came. The trees stood, powdered with white blossoming petals. We felt dizzy from this wild flowering. It is a very moment to break out into the spring whirlpool, breathe in, see enough, enjoy all the flowers that nature generously bestows on the earth. But instead, we were sitting in a tightly closed classroom, which had not yet had time to warm up with the spring rays. I just caught one of those rays, closing my eyes and spreading my wings. With half an ear, I listened to the professor's lecture, although it required full concentration because we had final exams and preparation for the thesis. Frankly, I did not understand how it happened that five years flew by like one year. I was filled with pleasant memories; I did not want to think about the future, which seemed very vague. The others had similar feelings. Alex and Ninel moved to the table in the last row and whispered about something non-stop as if they had got a common secret. They started spending more and more time together. No matter how Alex convinced himself and others that they were connected only by friendship, it was visible to the naked eye: Ninel's magnetism attracted him with irresistible force. Yuka kept her eyes on the bee that flew in through the open window, mistaking my friend's wings for an exotic flower. Our general relaxation was interrupted by a freshman. Sticking his head in the doorway, he loudly shouted in anticipation of the severe reprimand that awaited us, "The Fantastic Four, the rector calls you!"

We started up, throwing off the laziness and relaxation, and together stomped into the rector's office, while maintaining the dignity inherent to senior students.

Not only academic leaders gathered in the rector's office. Marina's dress stood out as a bright spot among the gloomy suits. Next to Marina was a young man, apparently of our age, who clearly fell out of the company of professors and functionaries. With all those present, we somehow crossed paths over the five years of study, and only this guy was seen for the first time. But it was he who stood up to shake hands with each of us. The stranger held himself confidently: they say about such people that 'they stand firmly on the ground.' My fragile hand literally sank into the strong palm of a plowman. Our eyes met, and it became clear that I was greatly mistaken about his age. Or he happened to see as much as we never dreamed of. Marina interrupted my fleeting observations:

"Guys, please meet: this is Stefan. He is a representative of the One World company and asked us for help. But let Stefan explain himself."

I looked into his eyes. They were light but so deep that there seemed to be no bottom in them. I wanted to look into them again and again. At the same time, Stefan himself looked at us openly and attentively, as if he wanted to immediately understand who we were and whether we could be trusted.

"Our organization is collecting biomaterial from representatives of different nationalities, trying not to miss any of the peoples inhabiting our planet. The idea is to create a special rapid test, by making which any person can find out where they originally came from and who their ancestors were. For example, the current inhabitants of Europe did not always live in this part of the world. There is exact scientific evidence that once upon a time, the progenitors of many of them were the population of Central America or Asia, and even Africa. In addition to the fact that the study is of an applied nature, it has an important humanitarian meaning. We want to show people that there are no immortalized owners of any island on earth. It belongs to all of us inseparably. We are at a development stage where an extensive database is required. Usually, we have no problems with collecting material: people themselves express their desire to participate in the project. But there are such hard-to-reach areas where scientists are deprived of the opportunity to conduct full-scale studies. Meanwhile, interesting in every sense, but little-studied ethnic groups live there. Such a region, of course, is the Pamirs. What do you know about Pamir?"

Ninel jumped off the seat first: she was eager to tell everything she knew.

"The Pamirs are called 'the roof of the world,' because the foothills of this mountain system are higher than the tops of other mountains. The Pamir Mountains really stand, as it were, on the 'roof.' Tibet is the only mountain range on the planet that rises steeper than the Pamirs. But the name 'the roof of the world' arose many centuries ago when people inhabiting Central Asia did not even suspect the existence of Tibet. However, this does not prevent the Pamirs from being a legendary geographical phenomenon located in the area of convergence of the highest ranges and mountain systems of the continent – the Kunlun, the Tien Shan, and the Hindu Kush. The Pamir Highway was part of the historical Silk Road that ran through the territories of Central Asia," Alex added. "This is a road full of unexpected turns and detours, and travelers still never get tired of putting them on maps."

"But Marco Polo described the Pamirs as the birthplace of water, a place where the sources of many rivers converge: the waters of the Amu Darya run in one direction, the tributaries of the Indus in the other," announced Yuka, who joined the conversation. "Thanks to the turbulent mountain currents, the valleys have excellent pastures. There is diverse wildlife, and you can meet rare animals. It happened with Marco Polo himself as well: he discovered a family of mountain sheep. Subsequently, this type of animal will be called the Marco Polo sheep."

And then everyone looked at me, waiting for what I would add to the topic.

"East Iranian, Tocharian and Dard tribes took part in the formation of the Pamir people," I said, believing that the most important thing in any science is knowledge about people. "Until the nineteenth century, the Old Vanch (Old Chinese) language was spoken on the territory of the Pamirs, which, unfortunately, is now completely lost. Now the Pamirs speak mainly Tajik and Kyrgyz. But, of course, each settlement has its own dialect, as well as its own unique destiny," I put the last point.

The teaching staff nodded favorably, satisfied with the results of their teaching activities.

"They are indeed savvy here," Stefan remarked, addressing either Marina or the entire Great Khural. Then he rapped out in a business-like manner, "I hope you will make up the route of our trip in such a way that we can cover the maximum number of settlements, including the most remote ones." This appeal, no doubt, was addressed specifically to us.

There was no time for slacking off. Stefan said that a helicopter is already being prepared, which will promptly pick up the collected material and deliver everything necessary to the route. Looking at each other, we happily nodded our heads. The offer was so tempting that the thought of refusing did not even cross our minds. It remained to get Marina's approval, and we looked inquiringly at her.

Marina, it seemed to me, said not without pride, "Stefan, you won't find a better team for your expedition. All support will be provided from the Academy to your mission – our curator assured."

"Wait, what about exams and theses? – After all, the expedition will take all our time!" Unexpectedly for myself, I got out with an untimely question, causing my friends to look at me, as if at an enemy who had crept into the ranks of the heroes.

"I think fellow teachers will be able to solve this dilemma. We'll figure out something," the rector summed up, slightly winking at the audience.

It was simply impossible to hide emotions here. We jumped off our seats and started hugging Marina, the rector and the professors, forgetting that just recently, we tried to stay as far away from them as possible. Marina coughed as if reminding us of this. A portion of our puppy joy went to Stefan. Finally, with the words 'We will not let you down,' 'We will try,' and 'Thank you for your trust,' we fell out of the office and rushed to Yuka's house. We couldn't wait to digest everything that had happened to us.

Chapter 11
Into the Deep of the Mysterious Region

We argued for a long time and could not come to a common opinion about the starting point of our expedition. The Pamir Highway passed through Kyrgyzstan, Tajikistan, and Afghanistan. For obvious reasons, we did not even think of going to Afghanistan, but we wanted to get as close as possible to its border. The key question was which geographical point to choose as a start – Kyrgyzstan or Tajikistan. During long hours of discussions, with Stefan's invariable participation, we finally decided on the route.

It looked like this:

Dushanbe – Kalai-Khumb – Khorog – Lyangar – Murghab – Karakul – Osh.

The starting point was the capital of Tajikistan, where, according to the plan, the whole group was supposed to fly. Then, in two jeeps, we will go deep into the Pamir region, where a fantastic highway awaits us. After all, the Pamir Highway is a part of the historical Silk Road, where every traveler dreams of getting to. But we clearly understood that we were not going on the road as tourists: we had an important mission ahead of us. Therefore, we were looking forward to incredible adventures and rapprochement not only with nature but first of all with the people of the Central Asian region, described by many travelers and at the same time, still fraught with many mysteries.

Only large settlements were indicated in the guidebooks, and our task was to find out the location of the kishlaks (mountain villages) on site, which we also had to put on the map.

In total, we had to walk and drive over a thousand kilometers. We prepared very carefully; it was important not to miss a single detail. In fact, there could be no minor items in the preparation of the expedition, and therefore everything was taken into account: operational communications, DNA sampling equipment, and various gears.

And now the route is approved by international curators. Backpacks are stuffed to the brim, we are standing early in the morning at the pick-up point, accompanied by relatives. Mom tries to hide her excitement, but the characteristic stroking of my back gives her away. She escorts me as if I go to war. We never parted for such a long time: I was leaving for three full months. Yuki's father wanted to make sure we had enough provisions, and just in case, he brought a watermelon in a shopping bag. In size, it could compete with a backpack. Yuka grumbled about that for a long time, but she took the watermelon.

We saw Ninel's parents for the first time. It was a very intelligent couple. It immediately became clear that we were facing a professorial family. Goth Ninel seemed to be their adopted daughter. Her parents looked at everything that was happening with extreme caution. Alex came up to them. I couldn't hear what he was saying to them, but after a couple of minutes, they were already smiling and confidently nodding in agreement.

Our loved ones did not want us to leave so much that they did not let us out of their arms for a long time. But then the car came: it was time to go to the airport. As I drove away, I looked out the window until my mother's silhouette disappeared into the morning mist.

We were ready for difficulties and when preparing, it seemed that we took into account all the technical issues that could come up during the expedition. But we could not imagine that we would face problems of a completely different nature. For example, the first weeks will be spent on gaining the trust of local inhabitants. They were very unfriendly to strangers. In each village, aul, kishlak, our acquaintance began with an explanation of why we are here. We had simple conversations with people about their everyday life, and somehow it became clear by itself that with their special lifestyle, they were able to tell something new about humanity. The peoples of the Pamirs, connected by roots with the ancient Scythians, have preserved their gene pool almost in its original form. Despite their isolation, their gene pool will be included in the common treasury of world values.

At some point, the rumor about young researchers ran ahead of us. Volunteers appeared who enthusiastically were helping us. Most of the time was spent identifying men who were not related to each other by family ties. For example, you cannot include father and son or grandfather and grandson in one list, since relatives have similar genotypes and do not provide additional information. And in other villages, it happens that everyone is related to each other by family ties – now you go and figure out which gene anyone has. So now, upon arrival at a new place, volunteers with ready-made lists were waiting for us.

Working conditions were often extreme. We worked till late at night, filling out questionnaires, taking photos of the participants of the experiment, and taking blood in the weak light of a flashlight. Stephen never stopped amazing me. It seemed that he could find a vein in an arm even with his eyes closed.

Many unexpected questions arose every hour. Some were solved on the go, others tormented and deprived of sleep. But, oddly enough, they did not bother me. On the contrary, we enjoyed interacting with people. Each one had a story to tell. Once we won the trust of the locals, they were not stingy in sharing their worries and aspirations with us. That hospitality of souls was more important than a richly served table; it gave strength and energy. The expedition had already lasted for two months, and there was no fatigue at all.

Often, we were surrounded by absolutely Martian landscapes. Sometimes for many kilometers of the route, we did not meet a single living soul. In complete silence, chains of hills and dunes stretched, behind which rocks resembling castles with high towers protruded. But, looking more closely through binoculars with special optics, we could see many real fortresses on the peaks. Who and when built them there remained a mystery. Historians and ethnographers have to look for a clue. We had to move along the route, not missing a single object inhabited by anything other than the shadows of the past. Only one person, who lived at the turn of the nineteenth and twentieth centuries, excited our imagination, only his image constantly haunted us. The 27-year-old lieutenant of the Russian army Eduard Kivekes, who by the will of fate found himself in the Pamirs, felt the helplessness and defenselessness of the highlanders in front of the outer world. Not only military service but also the desire to protect them became the reason for his 20-year stay in Turkestan.

The air here is too rarefied: neither people nor cars have enough of it. Even a small rise is difficult. Jeeps stall, and we can't start them from the first try. Huge animals with long shaggy hair graze near the thorny bushes, as if they were thrown to us from space. These are yaks, or Tibetan bulls, which actually can only be found in these lands. They lazily watch our futile attempts to cope with the cars. We can't wait until we arrive in Khorog. We need a reboot after a hard pass.

And now, after complete desertion, we are met by a noisy ancient city. In Khorog, we planned to take a day off and visit the local market. When we finally got to it, we were struck by the variety of goods: there are Iranian carpets, and Afghan coinage, and even videotapes with Indian films of all times. As if the magical mountain Simsim suddenly decided to share its treasures. I walked among the rows, feeling a pleasure plunging into the atmosphere of oriental bargaining. I wasn't going to buy anything in particular; I liked the process itself. Suddenly, Ninel jumped out in front of me with a carpet over her shoulder.

"Why do you need carpet?" I exclaimed in surprise. "Now we will have to carry it all the way with us!"

"I'm just sure it's a flying carpet," said my friend with conviction. She immediately unwrapped her acquisition and flopped it onto the dusty road. The pattern was really fabulous, and I understood why Ninel could not resist buying.

"Gela, you should definitely meet the seller of this masterpiece. He is an incredible character. He's like an old man Hottabych, nothing else," Ninel deftly rolled up her magic carpet and pulled me along with her.

A few minutes later, we were already standing in front of the merchant's shop. He was dressed in a typical Afghan attire: bloomers, a jacket was put on over a long shirt, and an all-season Afghan hat, called 'dushmanka' because the Afghan Mujahideen (dushmans) prefer this headdress, flaunted on his head. The new acquaintance looked at us quite friendly, squinting out of habit, as if from the bright sun. It was difficult to determine his age: due to the difficult climatic and living conditions, people here look much older than their years.

I greeted him in Pashto with a respectful bow of my head. I asked how the trade was going. He was clearly taken aback by the attention of the blond Pashto-speaking girl. Somehow, imperceptibly, a conversation began, I wanted to know as much as possible about his family. He was originally from the city of Mazar-i-Sharif in the Afghan province of Balkh. Several generations of his family were engaged in the carpets trade.

Now he buys products in Pakistan, India, and Iran – and once every three months, he brings his goods here, to Khorog.

In turn, I talked about our expedition and noted with regret that we could not pass the route through Afghanistan: it is clearly not the right time for studying the gene pool there now. Khorog is our closest access point to this troubled country. The Afghan thought for a moment, as if weighing whether to talk to these pretty girls about something serious. And then he suddenly opened up about his side business. And so, we learned that on the mountain pass, on the very border between Tajikistan and Afghanistan, there is a settlement few people know about. What its inhabitants do for a living – he does not care. He usually stops there on the way to Khorog, takes the list of purchases from them and delivers the orders on the way back. A passport is not required there, since this piece of land does not actually belong to any state. And then, an unexpected proposal came up. If we decide to go there, he will show on the map of his own make the location of this godforsaken village. Then the merchant added, with a sly glance at us, that there was no other such village in the whole world. He himself will stay in Khorog for a few more weeks, but if we take with us purchases for the villagers, they will accept us like ones of their family.

The venture was risky but very tempting. We promised to talk to our curator and give our decision the next day.

Chapter 12
A Man in the Cave

"You are nuts!" Stefan was yelling. He didn't even want to hear anything. "No, no and no! Khorog is the closest point to Afghanistan on the approved route. And let me remind you, I am responsible for you!"

"Hold up, Stefan." I tried, if not to get through to the mind of the international organization officer, then at least to interest him as a researcher, having support from our company. "Just imagine that it is the DNA of these people that will become the pearl of all the collected material of our expedition! Look, I've thought of everything. You and Yuka continue to move along the route: in this case, our deviation will not affect the execution of the plan. Me, Alex, and Ninel will make only a small detour and will catch up with you at Karakul (meaning a 'Black Lake'). We will take instruments for tests that do not require blood sampling. And even if something happens to us, we will get in touch by a sat phone. Although nothing unexpected should happen."

I was already desperate to persuade Stefan, but unexpectedly he agreed. Apparently, the curiosity of the scientist still prevailed over the caution. Or maybe he still had that spirit of adventurism.

We were quick to give our consent to the merchant. And after a short time, we left the city, overloaded with goods for the inhabitants of a mysterious place.

We wanted an adventure, and we got it.

Looking at the mark on the map, it was only a couple of days' trip to the settlement, listed as Ak-Tabrani. Closer to the evening, we began to look for a place to sleep. It was dangerous to build a fire on the side of the road, and even leaving the headlights on was risky. In the afternoon, we spotted a broken, but quite a frisky Mercedes, which tucked in behind us. No matter how hard Alex tried to break away from his pursuers, making unthinkable turns for this height and narrow gauge on the powerful Gelendvagen, the Mercedes relentlessly followed us. Finally, on the pass, we noticed something that looked like a cave. Alex stepped on the gas with all his might, squeezing everything out of the jeep that it was capable of. The sound behind us suddenly vanished. We realized that the shelter had safely hidden us, and without hesitation, we decided to arrange a campsite here.

But before we had time to drop our backpacks from our shoulders, something strange began to happen to Ninel. Nothing like that has ever been seen before. There was something predatory in her appearance. Her eyes burned, she was moving her head from side to side, sniffing the air, and muttering under her breath, "Not the time, not the time yet. Your time hasn't come…"

Alex and I froze in complete bewilderment, afraid to move. Suddenly, there was a pop – sharp, like a burst of

New Year's fireworks – and here they appeared, Ninel's wings. In the semi-dark cave, they looked like the black hole of infinity. And then it suddenly struck me: well, of course, Ninel is from the kind of psychopomps, or guides of souls, whose duties include escorting the recently deceased to the afterlife. Their role is not to judge the dead but simply to guide them to the other world.

Alex, trying not to frighten our friend, called, "Ninel, what happened? Did you see someone?"

It looked like he already knew this secret about his girlfriend.

"But for me, there's not a soul here," I said with my lips alone.

Ninel, still in a trance, slowly said, "Just the same, I saw the soul, but it is not the time for it to cross the bridge. We urgently need to find its owner."

We turned on the lights and frantically scanned every nook and cranny in the cave. What we saw was shocking. There was indeed a man in the cave. His pulse was hardly felt, there were many wounds on his body. Having a quick examination, I discovered that his leg and arm were broken.

It was necessary to act quickly.

"Ninel, what do you say – your 'patient?'"

She answered sharply, "No, not mine. On the other side, they are not waiting for him and are extremely unhappy with the invasion attempt. Apparently, he was unconscious for a long time, and his soul was lost between two worlds." Here comes Alex.

"While you talk about his soul, I will give him medical aid."

We laid the man on the Ninel's carpet, which turned out to be the most useful. We had to cut the victim's clothes, because of the gore, they stuck to his body. There was no living place on it, it was completely covered with wounds and abrasions. It was hard to imagine what happened to him and how he ended up alone in an abandoned cave. While Alex and I were doing the medical part, Ninel stood with outstretched wings, as if guarding the gates invisible to Alex and me. The sight was impressive and frightening at the same time.

And then Ninel offered me the role of a beacon of the soul. I did not really understand how it should work, but since there were no other ideas and there was nothing to lose in this case, I agreed.

Bending over to the victim, I tried to open my wings, but nothing worked. I didn't see or feel anything. Ninel began to get angry.

"We're wasting time. Man up!"

I was in despair: a man was dying in my arms.

"Gela," Alex spoke, "you are a leader, you are our beacon throughout all the years of study. This is who you are. Here and now lead the lost soul behind you."

I don't know what affected me more – Alex's words or Ninel's anger – I already knew what these inbeings were capable of. I put the victim's head on my lap, took his hands to read the pulse, and spread my wings. The cave suddenly became much brighter. At first, it seemed to me that Alex turned on an additional lantern, but then I realized that those were my wings. They were radiating light – flickering at first, like a lightbulb in an unstable voltage, but as the heartbeat became clearer, the wings glowed brighter.

And then the victim began to moan and cough, gradually regaining consciousness. He was muttering something unintelligible as he switched from English to French. I heard the characteristic pop again – and, looking at Ninel, I saw that her wings had disappeared. If Alex hadn't jumped up and caught her in time, she would have collapsed right to the ground.

Chapter 13
Racing with Mad Max

We were eager to continue our way the next morning. But our rescue was too weak for further movement. We tried to get in touch with Yuka and Stefan to report our delay, but the satellite signal was impossible to pick up. Meanwhile, the wounded man was still in deep oblivion, and only in the evening, it was possible to find out from his semi-delirium that he was a tourist from Britain named Henry Taylor. We hoped to find out later what kind of wind brought him to this place far from civilization. At least, it was clear through which services to look for his relatives.

We were sorely lacking communication with the world. At some point, we miraculously managed to break through, and I even heard Yuki's voice, but then it immediately disappeared. Having a 24-hour break, we finally got into the car and moved along the route. But we couldn't drive at high speed: off-road, the car shook like a cart, and we were worried about Henry. Although he was doing well, it did not go unnoticed for us how much pain each pothole on the road caused him.

From the moment we left the cave, I had the feeling that we were being watched. We drove in complete silence, but then Alex dropped, "So this is how an animal feels when a hunter is stalking it…"

"What are you talking about?" I asked.

"Oh never mind. Bad feeling."

Now we both began to look around carefully. We had to make a stopover to bandage Henry's wounds. The process dragged on as we rewound the ward like a mummy from top to bottom. Ninel unsuccessfully tried once again to get in touch with our advanced group. And then it dawned on me: we are under bearing. Yes, yes, the signal in the receiver was characteristic of wiretapping: each beep echoed as if it were being heard somewhere else in the parallel tube. I have no doubt left. Jumping up as if scalded, I sharply shouted:

"We must not lose a minute; we have to leave as soon as possible and rush to the village with all our might. We need to get out of here immediately!"

Nobody asked a single question. We didn't even manage to accelerate properly when the same Mercedes appeared on the horizon like a devil from a snuffbox. It was difficult to call it a car – rather, it resembled a vehicle from the Mad Max movie, and it behaved the same way on the road. Alex stepped on the accelerator pedal. It seemed that we managed to break away, but, apparently, the criminals in that car also understood this and opened fire on us. To say that this came as a complete surprise would be an understatement. None of us, in our wildest dreams, would ever have to fight someone like Mad Max. We did not panic, the nerves were like a string, and the brain worked clearly. Sharply turning the steering wheel, Alex pulled off the road. We won a few minutes. Leaving the car, we hastily put on backpacks, I winded up my head, leaving only my eyes open. My blonde hair could be very visible from a distance. We put Henry on a carpet and carried him on this a makeshift stretcher through the stone heaps into the mountains, avoiding pursuit. Everyone's wings were outstretched.

The day was drawing to dusk, coming darkness was our advantage. A canopy of heaven shone above us with a scattering of diamonds. Alex laid out a new route in his head, guided by the stars. There was no fear, there was a feeling of an endless universe above us. We believed that it would not leave us.

Henry was badly shaken during the day in a makeshift stretcher hammock, and, lying on solid ground, he finally came to life and told us his story.

Since childhood, Henry dreamed of following the route that his great-grandfather once walked. Great-grandfather led the work on the British side to build a route from India to Afghanistan. The exciting stories of the venerable old man, filled with the spirit of adventurism and challenges, forever sunk into the soul of a little boy. He grew up with a dream to repeat the path of his great-grandfather. And although the family was against it and in every possible way dissuaded from a rash act, immediately after graduating from the university, Henry nevertheless decided to fulfil his childhood dream. He went on a trip with his best friend. At first, everything went pretty smoothly. Without much difficulty, they overcame a many-kilometer path, and on the final stretch, they liked an unusual rock. It somehow magically attracted them. William – that was his friend's name – immediately refused the role of a conqueror and offered his services below. He stayed on the belay, and Henry climbed to the top and successfully reached it. But already on the descent, the D-link peeled off – and Henry flew down at a speed that did not even allow him to realize what was happening. Well, we all know well how it happens: we've been in such situations a few times. This happens in seconds. In such cases, your life depends on who insures you. It seems that William was not holding the safety lines securely and was unable to react quickly. Henry fell into a crevice and was badly injured. Actually, the fact that he did not die immediately was a miracle. William called him several times but could not get him out of the crevice. Through the pain, stunned from the fall, Henry barely heard that his friend had gone for help.

We tried to understand how Henry, caught between life and death, managed to get out of the crevice and get into the cave. Our rescued man could not say anything intelligible to that. He also did not understand how much time had passed since William had left him. From the condition of the wounds, it was clear that everything had happened about five days ago. The nearest village is less than a day's journey by car, and it will take not more than two or three days on foot. We didn't want Henry to be upset because of our comments. Tomorrow, we will be right in that village and find out for sure what happened to William.

Chapter 14
On the Edge of the Deep

So, quite openly, worrying only about the wounded Henry, we entered Ak-Tabrani, a village that seemed postapocalyptic. Time seems to have stopped in this region. One-story clay houses looked out onto the street through dark windows. And the streets themselves, in the absence of planning, formed a labyrinth. There wasn't any sign of electricity here – and no sign of food indeed.

We wandered along the winding path between the houses in the hope of meeting at least one living soul.

"Are they all dead or what?" Alex exclaimed emotionally.

Suddenly, a woman's figure appeared from behind a low duval. A dark scarf tightly covered her face and head, so it was impossible to determine the woman's age. For her, our appearance was so unexpected that she dropped the basin with washing from her hands, which she was about to hang for drying. For a moment, everyone froze. The stranger was the first to give a sign – cautiously looking around, she slightly opened the gate, inviting us into the house.

"Why, why did you come here, this is a bad place," the woman muttered, helping to lay down the wounded man. She seated us at the table and gave everyone water.

The woman spoke Pashto, so her lamentations were understandable to me. It was not clear why she was so nervous or whom she was afraid of.

"No place for you here, no place. Such young children, just like my Batyrchik was," continued the hostess.

I looked around. During our journey, we visited many houses, but this one was particularly poor. There was not even a curtain on the only window through which the morning sun barely penetrated. I only took a breath to ask the woman the questions that tormented us, when she abruptly ran up to the window, saw something or someone – and with a quickness that was hard to expect from her, pushed the table away and threw back something that looked like a rug. Beneath, there was a secret door that led to a tunnel.

"Hide all quickly!" the woman commanded in a whisper. There were such notes in her voice that we did not dare to argue.

Once in a deaf dark room, we heard several people burst into the room above us. From the loud clatter and ominous voices, it was easy to guess that those who had come here were by no means on a friendly visit. We could only hear snippets of phrases, but I could still make out a few words.

"Where are they? If we find out that you hid them, you will deeply regret it!"

The woman was stubbornly silent. The thudding continued for a while, then all was quiet. Meanwhile, no one was in a hurry to let us out of the dungeon.

The eyes finally adapted to the dark and began to distinguish peeling walls without windows and some faint light visible at the end of the tunnel. Our flying carpet was irretrievably lost, Alex took off his jacket and covered Henry. He was still very weak and immediately fell asleep. And we silently, as if spellbound, continued to catch a barely distinguishable ray of freedom from the abyss in which we found ourselves.

So much has happened over the past two days that we did not even manage to discuss her reincarnation with Ninel. It seemed to me that the right moment had finally come, and I moved closer to her. Ninel understood me without words and began her story.

NINEL

"You saw my parents. They are scientists and professors. All their lives they were only interested in work, there was always no time left for bringing me up. My grandmother took care of me. Do you think I regret that this is how my childhood turned out? Not at all. I was happy. After all, I got the coolest grandmother in the world! She could bake sweets, and go to the skating rink with me, and participate in the home theatre in the first roles. But suddenly, the grandmother fell ill and began to fade away right before our eyes. She practically did not get out of bed; it was clear how her strength was leaving her every day. I was afraid that I would go to school, I would return – and she would be gone. The thought that I would be left alone in the whole world deprived me of sleep and stole my rest.

I remember the day it happened like it was yesterday. I came home from school and immediately rushed to the room where my grandmother was lying. She seemed to be waiting for me to say goodbye. I took her hand and looked into her eyes.

I understood that the end was near, but I badly wanted to delay her at least for a little. I grabbed my grandmother's hand. But her soul was so tormented by the illness that it was impossible to keep it. I felt my grandmother's soul as something tangible, like her hand that I held in mine. Suddenly there was a pop – sharp. I did not immediately realize what had happened – and only looking back, I saw huge black wings behind me. Then everything was like in a fantasy movie. I looked at myself from the side: a winged teenage girl was holding her grandmother by the hand – cheerful, perky, the same as she was before her illness. Grandmother smiled and asked, 'Take me to the door, dear.' I seemed to know where to take her. There was a huge gate in front of us. On the other side, she has already been met. A moment later, I woke up again in my room, holding my grandmother's cold hand. My wings never appeared again, and I even believed that they appeared, like a phantom, as a result of my shock due to the loss of a loved one. A few years later, already at the Academy, when you all began to grow wings, the fear that mine were about to appear, increased every day. I was afraid to admit to myself that I am the black angel of death. Ninel finished with a sigh.

I put my arms around her.

"Why didn't you share it with us? You are not an angel of death, you are a guide. You help souls find their place: some obtain eternal rest, others – return to their master. I'm sure you and Alex are the perfect couple. He is a guide on earth, and you are on the other side of life. What you did for Henry, keeping him alive, no one else could do. We wouldn't have made it without you. You know, when my time comes, I'll be at peace knowing that you're holding my soul right."

Suddenly, Alex squeezed between us, tightly hugged us both to him and said in a low voice, "It's too early for us to say goodbye to our souls."

Chapter 15
SOS!

I came up with the idea of how to set us free. I believed even more that it could really happen when the floorboards creaked overhead, and our new friend finally let us out. She pointed us to a modestly served table. We were grateful to her for the treat and even more so for the salvation. Briefly, I told her the story of our adventures. She looked at everyone with some suspicion, but especially unkindly – at Henry. Finally, nodding in his direction, she said, "I saw his countryman. He was on the side of these criminals. He promised them a lot of money. He assured that he would soon get rich and that he had great connections in his homeland. Like to help them sell the 'junk.' Oh, they were so happy, jackals! All our children were ruined by their 'junk.' My son's name was Batyr, I wanted to send him away from here, to the city to relatives. No matter how I tried to save him, I didn't make it in time: He got burned out by their 'junk.'"

At that moment, I clearly understood what 'dry tears' were. This woman looked with eyes that had not cried for a long time, and in her eyes, the universal sadness from an irreparable loss was reflected.

Apparently, she kept the pain accumulated over the years for a very long time and was finally able to speak out. This effect, when complete strangers reveal their secrets to each other, knowing that these secrets will not go beyond the limits of the car, is often called the 'fellow traveler on the train.' We understood that our new acquaintance needed to remove that stone burden of pain and loss from her soul, so we did not interrupt her. She talked about all the horrors that this gang of thugs had done over the years. Trafficking in drugs, weapons and – the worst thing – human trafficking… They were not afraid of either human punishment or the punishment of the Almighty. As more and more details surfaced, horror seized my heart, fear fettered every cell of my body. It was hard to imagine that there are places on earth where people live much worse in the twenty-first century than in the Middle Ages. But hatred for these scumbags, the strive for justice and punishment prevailed. However, our priority now was our salvation. Allowing the mistress of the house to talk, I carefully brought the conversation to the implementation of the plan that had matured in my head.

"How did you know that the foreigner promised them?" I asked.

"Cause I'm their laundry lady. I go and collect their dirty stuff and wash the whole crowd. I hoped that my son would not be touched, I begged, but that devilish offspring had nothing sacred."

"How did the Englishman get out of here?" Alex asked.

"The helicopter flew in and took him away. And he personally called the helicopter, I saw it with my own eyes.

He took a radio set from those scumbags and called it himself."

"And when will you go for linen?" I clarified believing even more in the possibility of realizing my idea.

"I'll go tonight. Let's just decide what to do with you. You can't stay here!" the woman said.

I either believed that there was no need to delay and hastened to voice my plan. So, I'll go with her disguised as a distant relative. Moreover, it is difficult to identify a foreigner under closed clothes. During the months spent under the scorching sun and harsh wind, the skin on my face was so weathered and tanned that I could easily pass for my own. Everything is in order with my eyes: during the expedition, local residents said more than once that the emerald color of my eyes was very similar to the color of the eyes of true Pamiris. The problem was only with the hair, which was burnt out and looked like white gold: they could not be hidden under a scarf. But here our savior again showed enviable agility. She took some soiled bag from the shelf, on which I managed to make out the inscription 'Henna.' The woman quickly diluted the powder with water and applied it to my hair. Very soon, in a shard of a mirror, I saw how they darkened. After I rinsed my head out of the jug, all those present saw with admiration my transformation into a red-haired beast, which fully reflected my inner state. In general, I was ready to go on reconnaissance and, at the first opportunity, steal a walkie-talkie from the criminals.

Chapter 16
In the Lair of Jackals

It took no more than five minutes to assemble. The new hair color and my legend were supposed to help the plan. Before leaving, I hugged everyone, ordered them to leave the village in case of failure and an unforeseen situation, and make my way to my roundabout routes.

"And you, Henry, you would better play dumb. You understand, your people are not welcomed here," I said, ignoring all the rules of diplomacy.

Alex tried to object to me, but we were already leaving the house. In the confusion, we did not even have time to get to know the woman. My freshly baked aunt's name was Fatima. And when I introduced myself, she only shook her head in response – they say, no, the name Gela does not fit in any way.

The headquarters of the robbers who lived in these parts and controlled the village was located on the outskirts. According to Fatima, they occupied the abandoned stables, walking there for about thirty minutes. Along the way, we met local residents, and the 'aunt' would certainly explain to everyone, "My niece came to help me. Her name is Gul."

As a result, our journey dragged on for an hour. The closer we got, the more my heart pounded. Wings fluttered under the heavy black robe, begging to get out as if they wanted to carry me away from here.

The picture that came up to my eyes made me freeze. Of course, I did not expect that it would be a loft-style headquarters with all the amenities, but no one could have imagined that people could live in real stalls.

Most of the room was littered with some kind of boxes and was lit by the dim light of kerosene lamps. There was a smell of sweat in the air, either of the people who resided here or of the horses that once resided here. And the smell of something else, so familiar yet so elusive.

Fatima and I went from stall to stall and collected dirty laundry in a big bag. With a glance, I asked, "Well, where is this desired place of communication?" Fatima furtively pointed me to a room at the end of the corridor. Trying not to draw too much attention to myself, I moved towards the desired goal. None of those present paid any attention to us – what did they care about two women collecting their dirty laundry.

And here I am at the cherished door. I carefully opened it. Everything is going surprisingly smoothly. There is no one in the room, but there is no satellite communication tube either. But I saw the radio. Wasting no time, I sent the SOS signal and the coordinates to anyone who could take my call for help. I was so glad that everything went off without a hitch when suddenly the door burst open with a roar and a bearded man with a machine gun burst into the room. He blocked my exit. I froze in surprise. The man grabbed my arm and pulled me towards him. He bored me with his eyes, trying, like an x-ray, to enlighten me through and through.

"No, girl, you are not a niece. Our women do not look men in the eye, there is no humility in you. Or were you thinking of fooling us with this fancy dress?" He shook me as if he wanted to shake the soul out of me. "Well, tell me, who are you?" he growled.

I tried to pull away, but his hard hands, like a trap, held me in a stranglehold.

He shook me again and again as if trying to shake the answer out of me. My tightly tied handkerchief treacherously slipped over my shoulders, revealing short curls of hair. It was also impossible to hide the fire of hatred that burned in my green eyes. It was pointless to continue playing. I feverishly tried to assess my chances of escaping, but he dragged me along the corridor to the street, where Fatima had already been captured and, to my complete horror, Ninel, Alex and Henry were standing.

"All in the pit!" commanded the one holding me.

If it were a computer game, then at that moment, the inscription should have been displayed on the screen: GAME OVER = GAME OVER.

But it was not a game, and we had to fight for our lives to the end.

Chapter 17
'Salvation' Operation

And so we all ended up in a hole in the truest sense of the word. Apparently, that was the place where the criminals dumped their victims.

In the depth of night, the villains were noisily celebrating something, their barely coherent phrases reached the pit. We understood that nothing good could be expected from the onset of the morning and that we needed to act right now.

I told the guys that the original plan was not such a failure: I managed to send an SOS signal, but there was little hope that someone would receive it. So, the rescue of a drowning man is the drowning man's own job.

Although I would not say that our small team was in full combat readiness. Ninel was on the verge of panic. Alex was bent out of shape with impotence. My brain played over and over again everything I saw in that stable in order to find at least some clue. Bingo! Finally, I realized what that familiar smell was that I couldn't recognize right away. That had become our lifeline.

"So," I began, "we won't have a masquerade. We are who we are, and we need to take advantage of that. It will not be difficult for us to get out of this hole, it is not in vain that we spent so much time climbing walls. Henry will gather his strength now, and Ninel and I will help him, but Alex will have to pull Fatima out in a bundle. Gathering the straps and preparing the bundle," I commanded.

"Suppose we get out of here," Alex said skeptically. "And what then? In case you haven't noticed, there's a stable of thugs out there! Twenty people, no less!"

"Twenty-four, to be exact," Ninel remarked pessimistically. "Gela, we didn't seem to take a Rambo course at the Academy. Or did I miss something?"

"You're right," I agreed, ignoring my friend's ironic tone. "But look up: they didn't even put a guard on us. We are harmless children for them. But how wrong they are! When we get out of the hole, Fatima and Henry will move towards the valley: if anyone comes to rescue us, then landing is possible only there. Well, we will do what we must: we will get even with the gang and get rid of a possible chase. There are ammo boxes inside. At first, I did not immediately understand what was haunting me, but then I remembered: that smell has been familiar to me since childhood."

Even in pitch darkness, one could guess how Ninel's eyes widened. I hastened to reassure her.

"No, no, nothing like what you think. I don't sell weapons. Just as a child, I loved spending time with my uncle, my mother's brother – he is an avid hunter with us. So don't be surprised that I can tell a wolf track from a dog track. With the help of their own warehouse, we will blow this hornet's nest to hell!"

"And this seems to be our only chance for salvation," Alex supported me.

We had only to wait for the right moment: when the enraged criminals would calm down. And as soon as that happened, we began to act. After exchanging our trademark 'winged' greeting, we got down to business.

Again, I had to adapt my outfit to the current situation. And now my long skirt, as they say, with a slight movement of the hand turned into bloomers. All that was required for this was to throw the back of the hem forward and tuck it into the belt. I successfully dealt with that.

The full moon was our only witness and helper. And if it could, it would certainly be surprised by what it saw: dark moving figures suddenly appeared from somewhere out of the ground. At first, they resembled people, but gradually they became more and more like strange birds. Our wings were spread, our movements resolute. Alex clearly indicated to Fatima which way he and Henry should go. Our 'English patient' used all his strength to get out of the hole, and as soon as he climbed to the surface, he collapsed exhausted. Fatima had to literally drag him on herself.

"We'll catch up with you," I repeated to Fatima, trying to speak as calmly and convincingly as possible. Although up here, my plan no longer seemed so realistic and feasible. But it was also clear that there was no way back, we had nowhere to go, and the three of us began to make our way to the stable.

"Ninel, I remind you: as soon as the fire breaks out, you will slam all the doors and try to hold them as long as possible," I said very harshly. There was no need to repeat what Alex and I had to do: we clearly understood the sequence of our actions. Alex refrained from any parting words, only kissed Ninel tightly – and we went inside.

First, I had to collect all the kerosene lamps. And although we moved silently, it seemed that the rustle of our wings could be heard a mile away. I pointed out exactly where I saw explosive boxes. Approaching them, we spilled kerosene on the floor. But before setting it on fire, with a gesture that accepts no objection, I ordered Alex to urgently head for the exit. I hoped that it would take me no more than five seconds to throw a match into a black puddle, and that during that time, no one would wake up.

Alex vanished into the darkness without protest. By the rustle of wings, I knew that he was moving away. And then I began the countdown: 5, 4, 3, 2, 1 – and with the words 'burn in hell,' I set fire to spilled kerosene. The fire quickly engulfed everything around me, I immediately ran out of the stall and rushed to the exit. I left out one thing: gun oil and kerosene were everywhere and the flames spread like a fireball. The pungent smell of scorched feathers – my feathers – was overtaking me, and I panicked. To see what was happening behind me, I looked around sharply, but, stumbling over something hard, I lost my balance and fell right in the middle of this impossibly long corridor. Panic and horror seized me, making it difficult to soberly assess the situation. Covering my head with my hands from the unbearable heat, I began to say goodbye to my life. Suddenly, someone grabbed me in an armful and abruptly lifted me up. It was Alex.

"Did you really think that I would leave you? Come on, run!"

We rushed out of the stable just as the alarm went off. The inhabitants of the stalls tried to get out of them, but Ninel did an excellent job with her task and held all the doors, having previously blocked them with heavy objects – everything that came to hand. When it became clear that the criminals had no chance of escaping, Ninel lowered her arms and spread her wings. Together with Alex, they lifted me as my scorched wings barely fluttered in the wind. A favorable air current helped us move easily and quickly towards the valley, where Fatima and Henry were supposed to be waiting for us. It seemed to me that Alex was holding something heavy in his hands, but now there was no time for questions. We rushed over the earth, not once looking back at the burning stables with our tormentors.

The pre-dawn sky was lit up with fiery flashes, and the peals of exploding ammunition were carried throughout the neighborhood.

Only when we arrived at the agreed meeting place, did we take a breath. Our appearances, to tell the truth, were not the most heroic. My drooping wings hung behind me like the lines of a charred parachute. Ninel, who made so much effort to hold the exits for the retreat of the criminals, lost a significant number of feathers. Alex's wings weren't in the best condition, but he was smiling broadly as he held out his burden to me. I was ready to kiss him, but I left it to Ninel. Through all the trouble, he carried the radio station! I immediately began to beat SOS. Even if our signal is not received, the sounds of explosions are most likely already audible at the nearest frontier post.

Fatima ran out to us. She rushed to hug everyone, as a mother hugs her children after a long separation, and kept saying, "Alive! Thanks God, you are alive!"

I asked her how Henry was, she took me to the nearest boulder they were hiding behind. Henry was unconscious but breathing. I breathed a sigh of relief: all of them are in place.

Some time passed, and we began to recover from the shock.

"Am I hallucinating, or do you also hear the chirping of an approaching helicopter?" Henry finally came to his senses.

We turned our heads, trying to see the pinwheel in the sky. Fortunately, the helicopter did not take long to appear from behind the mountain, like a big iron bird. We jumped up and waved our hands to be noticed. The helicopter started landing. Before it had time to completely turn off the engine, the propeller was still spinning, and Yuka had already jumped out of there. All our adventures are behind us. We are saved!

Chapter 18
Destination – Home!

Only once we reached inside the helicopter, we were finally able to exhale. From the changing landscape in the porthole, it was clear that we were flying home.

Upon arrival, we explained to Yuka and Stefan where we got new additions to the team. Henry urgently had to be hospitalized. Fatima stayed with him, she did not leave a single step from his hospital bed. Stefan managed to contact Henry's relatives through the embassy, but they could not fly right away. While Henry was in the hospital, I tried to spend all my free time with him. I wanted to know the details of the incident in the mountains. From fragments of his memoirs, I tried to make a complete picture of what happened. It turned out that after Henry fell from the cliff, William took him to the very cave where we found him and said that he was leaving for help. Henry was sure that he would definitely return, we just got ahead of him. I did not begin to tell about William everything that I learned from Fatima. We passed the information to the relevant authorities, and now they were investigating William's relations with the Afghan drug traffickers. And I really hope he gets what he deserves.

Talking about us, the events in our lives changed with lightning speed. We had barely had time to take a breath, when the day of graduation came. Down from a mall, straight to the ball, as they say. The female part of our fantastic four risked being left without evening gowns. Luckily, Yuka had a closet full of clothes for every taste, and with a grand gesture, she invited us to her personal boutique.

I didn't have to choose for a long time: I immediately laid eyes on the airy pink chiffon dress. It resembled cotton candy, which I have loved since childhood. Ninel did not give up her principles and chose a black floor-length dress made of dense satin.

Happy with successful home shopping, we put on the final touches of makeup.

"Well, Yuka, and what are you going to wear?" Ninel asked, turning in front of the mirror.

"Now you will see," Yuka answered mysteriously from behind the open cabinet door, which served as a screen. Finally, the victorious cry of a friend 'Ta-dam!' and she appeared before us.

Ninel and I froze in amazement. Yuka was wearing jeans and a white T-shirt. But those were not ordinary, but our legendary jeans. Yuka put them on more than once on joint trips, and often out of boredom in the evenings by the light of a flashlight, we painted them with wonderful pictures. On them, each of us painted our wings at the moment of their appearance. These jeans were historical and fateful for us.

"Voila. What do you think?" A friend was waiting for our approval.

"I can't speak at all, because now I'm going to cry and my mascara will flow!" With difficulty holding back tears, I opened my arms for a hug. Ninel joined us, clinging tightly with her wings. We stood like that for a few moments, realizing for the first time that a long separation awaited us.

Finally breaking away from each other, we hurried to the Academy, where Alex was already waiting for us.

How quickly and inexorably time flies! We felt it especially well, standing on the steps of our native Academy which became second home for us. It seemed that quite recently, fledgling teenagers, we timidly opened the doors, wondering with fear what awaited us ahead. And now we are in the same place, in the same composition, but already completely different: we boldly look forward, knowing that in any situation, our wings will support us.

"Well, who goes where? Diplomas are in hand, the floodgates are open," I said, not knowing how to start a farewell conversation. But it seemed that everyone was ready for it.

"Ninel and I will go to my village," Alex confidently answered for two, tightly hugging our friend by the shoulders.

"And I..." Yuka stammered with uncharacteristic timidity. "Well, I will go with Stefan to Tibet. He offered to continue the expedition with him," Yuka said, as if embarrassed. Although there is nothing to be ashamed of – everything showed that they were in love with each other, and one could only guess what happened between them while we were fighting the criminals.

But I was happy for everyone.

"I'm going to the Dominican Republic. I was asked to lead a new tourism project in the Dominican Republic from the Academy. Something like a 911 service for tourists. A business trip for a year."

"That's cool! You will live on a paradise island. We will fly in to visit you," everyone vying with each other began to congratulate me.

Before leaving for the miracle island, I went to say goodbye to Henry. His grandmother flew to visit him. The daughter of a famous traveler, she herself was not timid. Assessing the situation, the grandmother immediately decided to take Fatima with them.

"Well, Henry, it was nice to meet you, even under such strange circumstances. Maybe we'll meet someday somewhere." I nodded goodbye to him and hurried to leave the hospital. During the time that we spent together, especially when we were in dangerous troubles, I felt that I was becoming more and more attached to Henry, starting to hopelessly drown in the blue of his eyes. And now is not the right time to lose your head in love, because I have a lot of things ahead of me, a new country, a new life.

Epilogue

The voice of the captain of the aircraft, announcing the upcoming landing, brought me out of a deep trance, in which I found myself thanks to dear memories. I slammed the book I hadn't started reading and stuffed it into my bag. Suddenly, a photograph fell out of it, which Stefan took on the porch of the Academy right after the graduation. The photo was taken on a Polaroid, and by some miracle, our wings were displayed on it. After taking another look at the picture, as if saying goodbye to my friends, I hurried to put it in my bag so that no one could see the images.

Going down the stairs of the plane and breathing in the humid tropical air of a new country, I had a feeling that my future life here would be full of adventures no less than my student years at the Academy. And new stories and adventures will not take long to manifest.

9 798889 107620